# EL LAGO DE LA LUNA

# EL LAGO
# DE LA LUNA

Un relato de Ivan Gantschev
Traducido por Guillermo Gutiérrez

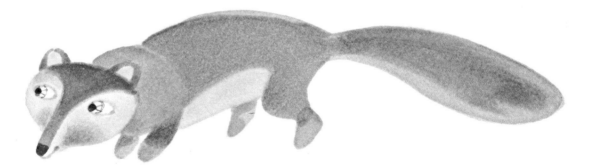

Ediciones Norte-Sur / New York

Lejos, muy lejos, oculto entre las montañas, había una vez un lago de aguas cristalinas. Las montañas que lo rodeaban eran tan altas que los profundos cañones eran oscuros como la noche. Pero a pesar de esto, el lago brillaba en el fondo con un fulgor de estrella.

La gente del lugar lo llamaba el Lago de la Luna, y cuenta la leyenda que la luna bajaba a bañarse en sus aguas heladas. Después del baño, cuando la luna se sacudía las gotas, una lluvia de piedras de plata caía sobre la orilla.

Muchos habían salido en busca del legendario lago, pero siempre en vano. Y algunos nunca regresaron, perdidos para siempre entre los desfiladeros.

Sólo un viejo pastor que vivía en lo más alto de las montañas conocía el lugar secreto. Su pequeña cabaña estaba a un día y una noche de camino del pueblo más cercano, y para alcanzarla había que atravesar densos bosques y trepar por escarpadas colinas. Nadie recorría el difícil camino y el pastor llevaba allí una vida sencilla, cuidando sus ovejas junto a su nieto Pedro.

Un invierno, cuando los senderos habían desaparecido bajo la nieve, el viejo pastor ya no pudo ocuparse de sus animales. Entonces se quedó junto al fuego mientras Pedro lo cuidaba y se encargaba de las ovejas.

El día más frío de aquel invierno, la vida del viejo pastor comenzó a apagarse. Cuando Pedro fue en busca de leña, el pastor se quedó mirando las brasas del fuego, y recordó el brillo de las piedras del Lago de la Luna. Había sido su intención mostrarle a Pedro el camino al lago, pero cuando el fuego se apagó, el pastor murió y el secreto del Lago de la Luna se perdió.

Pedro se quedó a vivir en la cabaña. Se
sentía feliz a pesar de estar solo. Las ovejas
le daban abundante leche para hacer el
queso que vendía en el pueblo. Con las
manzanas, las peras y las frambuesas
silvestres preparaba mermelada, y con las
cebollas, los ajos y la lechuga que cultivaba
y los hongos y las hierbas que encontraba
hacía deliciosas sopas calientes.
Una tarde, mientras llevaba sus ovejas al
corral, se dio cuenta de que faltaba una.

Pedro puso un trozo de pan y un pedazo de queso en una bolsa y salió en busca de la oveja perdida. Ya anochecía cuando llegó a un profundo cañón y escuchó un balido lastimero que parecía salir del fondo. Asomado al borde del precipicio, Pedro vio un lago de aguas tranquilas y relucientes. Allí, en la orilla, estaba su pobre oveja perdida.

Pedro encontró un sendero entre las rocas y descendió. Mientras bajaba, salió la luna e inundó el cañón con una luz brillante como el día.

La orilla del lago estaba cubierta de piedras plateadas que relucían a la luz de la luna.

—¡Qué piedras tan hermosas! —susurró Pedro asombrado, mientras recogía algunas y las guardaba en la bolsa.

—Si las vendo en el pueblo podré comprarme una manta y una camisa nuevas. Hasta podría comprar campanitas para ponérselas a las ovejas y saber dónde están... —se dijo.

—Sí, siempre y cuando encuentres el camino para salir de aquí —le replicó una voz a sus espaldas.

Pedro se dio vuelta y vio a un magnífico zorro plateado.

—Tengo mucha hambre —le dijo el zorro—. ¿Tienes algo de comer?

Sin dudarlo, Pedro le ofreció lo que llevaba.

El zorro devoró todo con ansia y le dijo:

—Para agradecerte lo que has hecho por mí, te confiaré el secreto del Lago de la Luna. Debes abandonar este lugar antes del amanecer, porque cuando salga el sol, el brillo de las piedras te cegará y ya nunca podrás encontrar el camino de vuelta. Sígueme, te mostraré cómo salir de aquí.

Pedro se echó la oveja a la espalda y, con la ayuda del zorro, encontró pronto la salida del cañón. Se despidió de su nuevo amigo y llegó a la cabaña sano y salvo antes del amanecer.

Poco después, Pedro recorrió el largo camino hasta el pueblo y se sentó a vender las piedras preciosas en el mercado. Apenas las había puesto sobre una tela, cuando llegaron los soldados del rey y le ordenaron que los siguiera al castillo.

El rey quería saber de dónde había sacado esas brillantes piedras, y Pedro le contó la historia. Entonces, los soldados le quitaron las piedras y el rey le exigió que le dijera dónde estaba el lago misterioso. Pedro no supo explicarle el camino. Cuando, nervioso, comenzó a tartamudear, el rey amenazó con echarlo a un profundo pozo lleno de serpientes si no le decía inmediatamente cómo llegar al lago.

A Pedro no le quedaba más remedio que guiar al rey y a sus hombres hasta el Lago de la Luna. Cabalgaron durante toda la noche y durante todo el día siguiente. Finalmente, al caer la noche llegaron al cañón. Mientras todos descendían por el desfiladero, la luna se elevó en el cielo y bañó las orillas del lago con su hermosa luz.

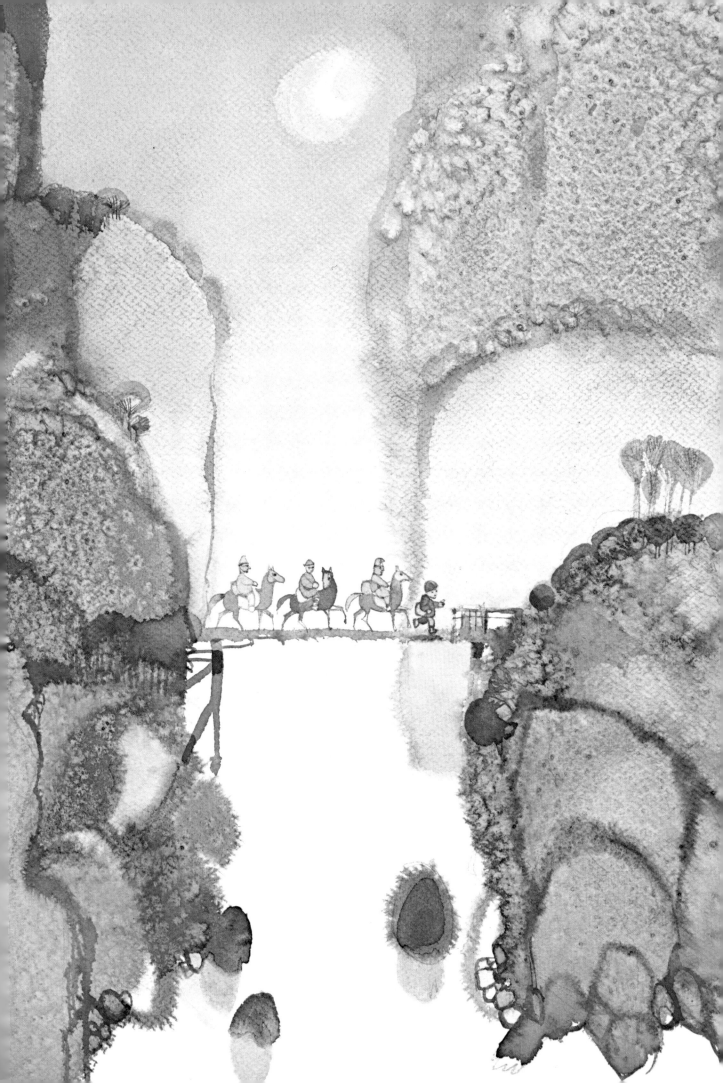

Inmediatamente, el rey y sus hombres empezaron a recoger
las relucientes piedras. Pedro no tomó ninguna y observó con
incredulidad cómo los hombres llenaban sus bolsas poseídos
por la codicia. De repente, recordó las palabras del zorro.
—¡Majestad! ¡Majestad! —le dijo al rey—. ¡Tenemos que salir de
aquí antes del amanecer, o la luz del sol nos cegará!
—¡Fuera de aquí! —le respondió el rey, encolerizado—. ¡Cómo
te atreves a decirle al rey lo que tiene que hacer!
Sin decir una palabra, Pedro se marchó dejando al rey y a
sus hombres a orillas del Lago de la Luna.

Cuando salió el sol, los hombres quedaron ciegos por el fulgor de las piedras. Cargados con las pesadas bolsas, intentaron avanzar a tientas entre las paredes del desfiladero, pero acabaron por precipitarse al fondo del abismo unos encima de otros, junto con sus piedras preciosas.

Como nadie había visto al rey y a sus hombres salir del castillo, nadie supo jamás qué había sido de ellos. El Lago de la Luna, resplandeciente como siempre, guarda el secreto.

Pedro volvió al lago sólo una vez más, a recoger algunas piedras.
Se las llevó a la cabaña y le puso una en el collar a cada oveja.
Desde entonces ninguna volvió a perderse, ya que su brillo podía
verse incluso en las noches más oscuras.
Pedro dejó en la ventana las piedras que le sobraron. Cuando hay
luna llena, las piedras brillan con tal fuerza que el joven pastor puede
trabajar bajo su luz toda la noche. Y cuando su amigo el zorro viene
de visita no tiene más que seguir el rastro de luz para encontrar la
cabaña, brillante y luminosa, en lo alto de la montaña.

# 6 PROJECT

# Square Flower Vases

Decorate these ultra-modern vases with colored gels that form a three-dimensional mix of iridescent shades and rich textures. Pattern and texture are built up on the outer surface of the vase, then left to dry to a hard finish that resembles molded glass.

## You will need

**iridescent green**
**opaline green**
**iridescent**
**ocean**
**iridescent silver**
**aquamarine**
**iridescent blue**

**Square tank vases**
**Gel paints, such as Gel**
**Crystal, as shown**
**Medium-sized flat**
**brush**
**Palette knife**
**Stiff card**
**Kitchen paper**

1 Clean the vase thoroughly. To achieve the three-dimensional effect, work on one side of the vase and let it dry to a hard finish that won't smudge when you turn it over to work on the other side. Randomly squeeze some of the ocean gel near one edge of the vase. Using the brush, spread the gel out over most of the side of the vase.

**2** Squeeze some of the darker blue gel near the lower edge of the vase. Using the palette knife, spread this out to form a uniform layer while merging some areas of the two colors together.

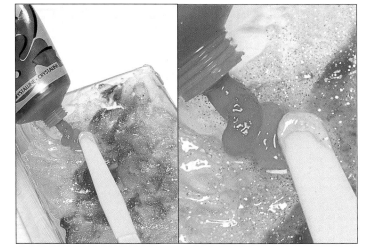

**3** Build up the surface with aquamarine, using the palette knife as before. The sides of the vase can be decorated in the same way with a selection of the colors shown on page 43, or they can be further embellished, as shown opposite.

**4** For a regular wave pattern, scrape through the gel with a comb cut from a piece of stiff card. Start at the top left-hand corner and pull the comb through the gel with a scalloping action. When you reach the right-hand side, lift off the comb and wipe away the excess gel with kitchen paper. Repeat this until the surface of the vase is covered with the wave texture. When you have completed one side of your vase, set it aside to dry, then repeat the process with the other three sides in turn.

## Variation

Add glass nuggets as focal points in the textured surface. Use two or three nuggets in a random arrangement, choosing colors that complement the gels. Place each nugget on the surface of the wet gel, then push it down onto the surface of the glass without disturbing the surrounding gel. The gel will dry to form a neat seal that holds the nugget in place.

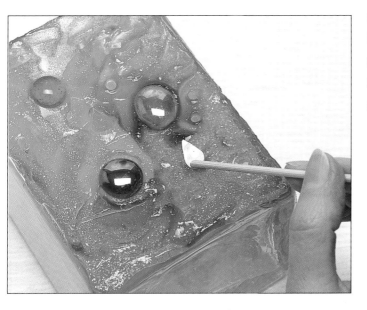

Clear acetate shapes can be added to create small windows in the gel. Use a hole-punch to cut out perfect circles of acetate or use scissors for larger shapes. Arrange the pieces of acetate on the surface of the wet gel, then use a cocktail stick or pencil to press them through the gel onto the surface of the glass. The rim of gel will hold the acetate in place.

The detail shows the dramatic effect of the combination of gels, glass nuggets and acetate. Try this technique on a night-light holder for a change.

G lass-sided lamps that hold candles and night lights are perfect for summer dining on the patio or in a garden or conservatory. Decorate the plain glass to match garden cushions or crockery and create a colorful, glowing light source. The design works equally well on a round lamp and on one with straight glass sides.

## You will need

**turquoise**
**yellow**
**crimson**

**Hurricane lamp**
**Colored wax pencil**
**Narrow masking tape**
**Craft knife**
**Transparent**
**glass paints**
**Palette**
**Small pieces of**
**synthetic sponge**
**Relief outliner in silver**
**Appropriate thinner**
**for cleaning brushes**

*1* If you can remove the glass from the lamp it will be easier to work on it. Release the glass cylinder or the individual glass panels from the frame and clean thoroughly. Insert back into the frame, draw along the edge of the frame with a wax pencil as shown, so that you can easily see the area to be decorated, then remove again.

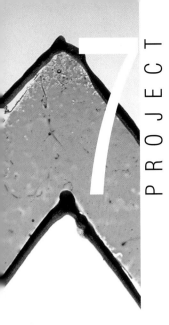

2 Measure and mark a central diamond shape on the glass with the wax pencil and mask it off with the masking tape. Then leave a gap and form an outer diamond border with another strip of tape. Use the craft knife to trim the tape into points where the ends overlap, then run your finger over the tape to make sure the edges adhere firmly to the glass.

3 Pour a little crimson paint into the palette and dip one side of a piece of sponge into the paint. Dab off the excess paint on the palette, then sponge the color onto the central diamond shape. Aim for an even coating without using too much paint which could seep under the masking tape.

4 To color the diamond border, repeat the sponging process with a clean piece of sponge and the turquoise paint.

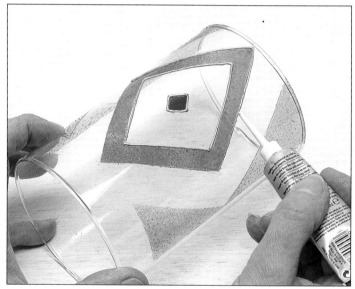

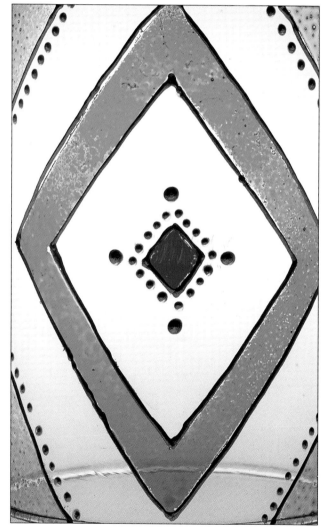

5 Sponge the outer area in the same way, using the yellow paint and a clean piece of sponge. Leave to dry. Carefully peel off the masking tape to reveal the finished pattern. If you have problems peeling it off cleanly, cut around the edge of the tape with the tip of the craft knife so that you slice through the layer of paint before removing the tape.

6 Trace the edge of each shape with the silver outliner. The outlines will emphasize the design and also cover any slight flaws on the edges of the paint.

7 Use the silver outliner to decorate the outline of the inner diamond and the inside of the diamond-shaped frame with rows of dots.

# Blue and Gold
# Glassware

H and-decorating a random collection of dark blue glass makes a spectacular set reminiscent of expensive Venetian glassware. This simple design with its richly contrasting colors has maximum impact. With a little practice, squeezing the outliner through the nozzle will produce pleasing results that require very little artistic skill.

## You will need

**outliner in gold**

**Blue wine glasses, tumblers and empty mineral water bottle**
**Masking tape**
**Ruler**
**Pencil**
**Outliner, as shown above**
**Plastic-topped cork that fits the bottle (optional)**

*1* Clean the glassware thoroughly. Wrap a piece of masking tape around the top of one of the wine glasses and trim it to the circumference of the rim. Remove the tape and place it on the work surface. Use the ruler to divide the strip of masking tape into eight equal sections and mark these with the pencil along the lower edge. Replace the tape round the top edge of the glass.

painting glass/project 8

PROJECT

**2** Use the gold outliner to draw diamond shapes onto the glass. The top point of each diamond should match up with the marks on the tape. Start with the outline of the diamond, then spiral in toward the center to fill the shape with gold.

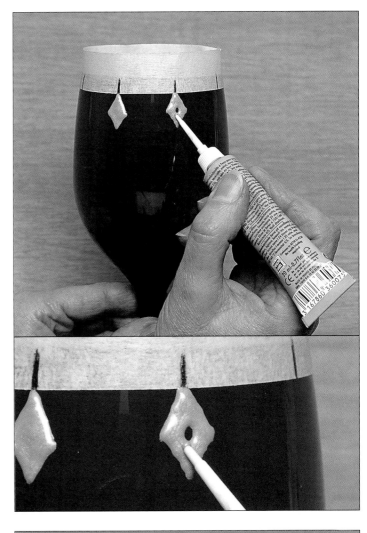

**3** Make a large dot centrally between each diamond, using the gold outliner. Then go around the glass again adding four small dots around each large dot.

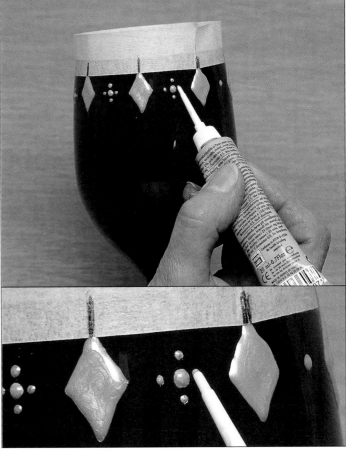

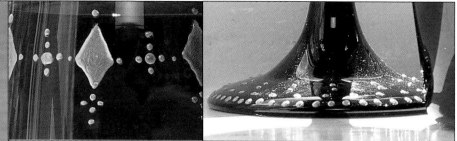

**4** Carefully remove the masking tape from the glass. (You can use it again on a matching glass.) Make four dots around each diamond, using the gold outliner, then add four dots below each diamond. Decorate the foot of the wine glass with rows of gold dots. Repeat the process with the remaining wine glasses.

**5** Follow the same method for the bottle and tumblers and decorate them with similar gold diamonds and dots. Wrap masking tape around the bottle and divide it into equal sections to position the diamonds.

**6** If you wish to make a stopper for the bottle, decorate a plastic-topped cork from a sherry or port bottle with lines and dots of gold outliner. When all the glassware has been decorated, bake it in the oven (omitting the plastic-topped cork) following the manufacturer's instructions.

### artist's tip

If you want to draw an accurate pattern for a more complex design using conical tumblers, make a paper template by rolling the glass across a sheet of paper. As you do this, draw a line that follows the top and bottom edges of the glass. Cut the shape out, wrap it around the glass and trim the ends of the paper so that it fits into the glass exactly. You can now use this to create more adventurous repeat patterns to trace onto the glass itself.

# Flora and Fauna
# Gallery

Top shelf, left to right:

**Stoppered Bottles** (Artist: Annette Malbon)
All these bottles are decorated using outliner and paints which the artist mixes herself from pigment and transparent base paints to achieve a wide range of vibrant colors.

**Vine Jug** (Artist: Vikki Miller)
The jug is decorated with an impressive grape vine motif. This should be drawn in black outliner from a tracing taped to the inside of the jug and then painted in rich colors.

**Color Combinations** (Artist: Vikki Miller)
This floral vase is painted with simple hand-drawn black outlines which are then filled in with a small brush, using alternating oil-based colors.

**Bright Dots**
The flower centers and the entire design on the blue and yellow jug were created by dipping cotton buds into paint and dabbing them onto the glass to make perfect dots each time.

Bottom shelf, left to right:

**Stemmed Glass** (Artist: Annette Malbon)
This delicate blue-and-pink flower pattern suits the shape and color of the glass. Look around and let yourself be inspired by the glassware you find, as this artist does.

**Ducks and Frogs** (Artist: Annette Malbon)
Outliner and bright green and yellow paints were used to create the jolly designs on these glasses. You could use different designs and colors to customize glasses for seasonal or other special occasions.

**Perfect Petals**
The wide petals on the glass are made with a round brush used flat on to the glass. The thinner petals on the jug (far right) were painted using only the tip of an angled brush.

**Bold Bloom**
A bold jungle flower is first drawn in black outliner and then filled with vivid pink and violet. The leaves are painted in emerald paint to create this exotic glass.

**Two-tone Jar** (Artist: Vikki Miller)
This is painted using the same technique as the small floral vase above.

# Candle and Tea-light Holders

P lain glass candle and tea-light holders can be turned into elegant, bejewelled creations that would grace the smartest dining table. The larger candle holder is embellished with glass nuggets in rich jewel colors, while smaller "jewels" are simply painted onto the tea-light holders.

**Safety note: Never leave lighted candles unattended.**

## You will need

**crimson**

**turquoise**

**emerald**

**lemon**

**gold**

**outliner in gold**

**Clear glass candle holder and tea-light holders**
**Narrow masking tape**
**Water-based paint, such as Porcelaine 150, as shown above**
**Palette**
**Small pieces of synthetic sponge**
**Outliner, as shown above**
**Glass bond adhesive**
**Glass nuggets in jewel colors**
**Small round brush**
**Masking fluid**
**Transparent paints in jewel colors**

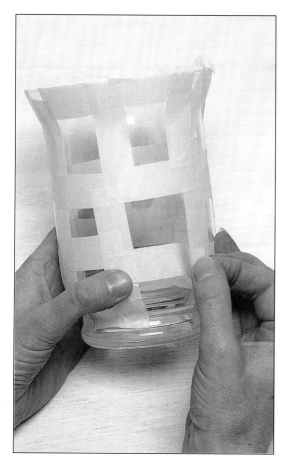

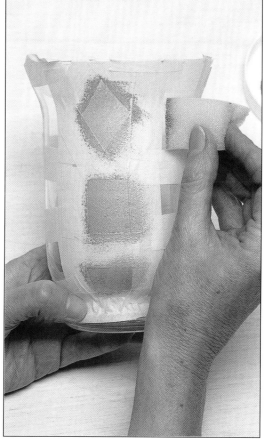

*1* Clean the holders thoroughly. Use strips of masking tape to mask a pattern of squares, diamonds and rectangles all around the candle holder. Arrange the shapes vertically in groups, with about three shapes in each group.

*2* Pour some gold paint onto the palette and dip a piece of sponge into it. Dab off any excess paint on the palette, then sponge the color onto the masked shapes. Leave to dry, then apply a second coat for maximum coverage.

**3** Remove the masking tape. Using gold outliner, draw lines around both sides of each shape, linking the shapes in each vertical group. Work carefully to avoid smudging the paint. Leave to dry until hard.

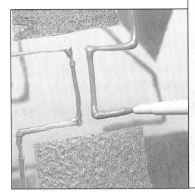

**4** Finally, use the glass glue to stick the nuggets onto some of the gold shapes. Work with the candle holder flat on the work surface and leave each nugget in the sunlight until the glue is dry before turning the holder to work on the next one. This will prevent the nuggets slipping off while the glue is wet.

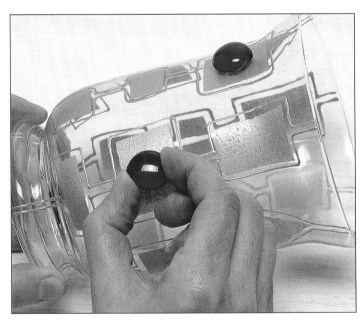

**5** For the tea-light holders, use strips of masking tape to mask about five shapes around each holder. Using the brush, paint a circle of the masking fluid in the center of each shape. Leave to dry.

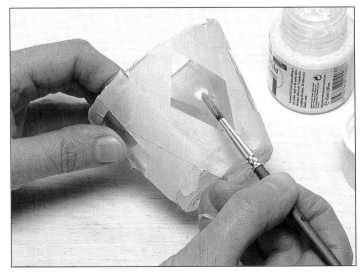

**6** Sponge the shapes with one or two coats of gold paint, as in step 2, and leave to dry completely.

## artist's tip

If you wish to add color to an item, paint the base with a glass paint. If the glass is quite thick the color will reflect up the sides without adding to the pattern or spoiling the design.

**7** Remove the tape and draw gold outlines, as in step 3. Leave to dry completely, then rub the masking fluid off the center of the gold shapes with your fingertip. Bake the candle holder and tea-light holders in the oven following the manufacturer's instructions. Paint the central circles inside the gold shapes on the tea-light holders with the jewel-colored paints, then leave to dry.

# Swedish-style
# Wine Glasses

Delicate, classic designs are stencilled and painted onto simple wine glasses in a charming Swedish style. Although the technique is subtle, it is very effective and can be adapted and used on many different-shaped glasses, jugs and decanters.

## You will need

matte medium

Acetate stencil sheet
(Mylar®)
Fine, black, waterproof
felt-tip pen
Thick card or
cutting mat
Craft knife
Plain wine glasses
Pencil
Stencil mount
Matte medium,
as shown
Palette or small dish
Small stencil brush
Small round brush

*1* Clean the glasses thoroughly. Cut two squares of acetate and use the felt-tip pen to trace the templates on page 92 onto them. Place the acetate on the thick card or a cutting mat, then use the craft knife to cut out the designs. This makes the stencils for the large and small motifs.

*2* Hold the stencil for the large motif in position on one of the wine glasses. Ensure the central line is vertical, then use the pencil to draw a line on the stencil that follows the rim of the wine glass. This will help you to position the design accurately on the glass.

*3* Spray the reverse of the stencil with stencil mount, then leave to dry until tacky. The adhesive will hold the stencil in position on the shiny, curved surface of the glass while you work.

*4* Position the stencil on the glass, lining up the pencil line with the rim of the glass. Pour a little matte medium onto a dish and dip the tip of the stencil brush into it. Dab off the excess on scrap paper, then dab a thin coat of the medium over the stencil. Leave to dry for a few moments, then peel off the stencil. Stencil the other glasses in the same way.

**5** Prepare the stencil for the small motif, as in step 3. When the large motif is quite dry, stencil small motifs around the rest of the rim of the wine glass, spacing them evenly. Leave to dry. Stencil the other glasses in the same way.

**6** Using the small brush, paint small dots of the medium onto the glasses to link the stencilled motifs. Leave to dry, then bake in the oven following the manufacturer's instructions.

*artist's tip*
If medium (or paint) accidentally seeps under a stencil, wait until it is touch-dry and then use the tip of a craft knife to carefully scrape away the excess. When you have corrected the shapes, leave the glasses until the medium is completely dry, then bake them in the oven following the manufacturer's instructions.

# Lightcatchers
# Gallery

This page:

**Christmas Decorations**
Small triangles of glass were painted with transparent colors inside gold outlines. Trees and stars are simple to do and you can choose a color scheme to go with the rest of your decorations. Glue narrow braid around the edge of each triangle when it is dry and make loops to hang them from festive garlands, at the window or from the branches of the Christmas tree.

Opposite page:

**Hearts, Stars and Abstract Patterns**
Most of these lightcatchers are made using the same basic method as shown on page 37-39. Start with a traced outline design which is drawn onto the glass using outliner in black, dark grey or a different color. When this is dry, paint each area in a different color using a selection of transparent paints.

**Pale Shades**
To achieve a different effect, as on the lightcatcher with the pale blue pattern (center), first sponge through a stencil and outline the design later.

**Fairytale on Glass** (Artist: Sue McIldowie)
The large lightcatcher with the complex design is decorated with flowers, fruit and birds, ideal for a child's room. Hang it from the window to show off the wonderfully vivid colors and fairytale design.

All the lightcatchers are hung up with braid glued around the edge or thread looped through a hole in the top.

# Rainbow Jug, Tumblers and Bowls

S imple but effective, this easy technique, combined with stunning colors, makes a set of glasses and dishes that would be great for a children's party or a summer dining table. The mosaic-like squares are painted with a single brush stroke and the rainbow colors can be adapted to go with your decor. The molded lines on the glasses used in this project help to keep the squares level, but the decoration can just as easily be painted freehand.

## You will need

**Ming blue**
citrine
**Parma violet**
saffron
**turquoise**
coral
**emerald**
ruby

**Glasses, fruit bowls
and jug**
**Water-based paints,
such as Porcelaine
150, as shown above**
**Small flat brush**
**Spare piece of glass
to practice on**
**Medium-sized
flat brush**

*1* Clean the glasses thoroughly. Arrange the paints in the order in which you will use them, remembering how one color leads on to the next in a rainbow. Start with emerald, then turquoise, blue, Parma violet, ruby, coral, saffron and citrine.

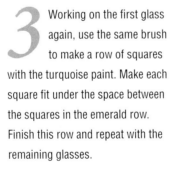

2 Using the small, flat brush, try painting even squares on a spare piece of glass by making a single short brush stroke for each one. Then, starting with emerald, paint evenly spaced squares diagonally around the base of one of the glasses. Leave to dry while you paint the next glass in the same way. Repeat the process with all the glasses.

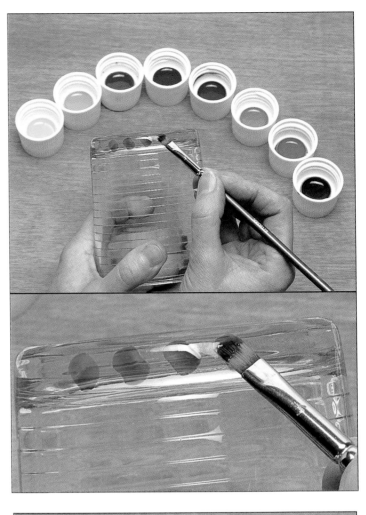

3 Working on the first glass again, use the same brush to make a row of squares with the turquoise paint. Make each square fit under the space between the squares in the emerald row. Finish this row and repeat with the remaining glasses.

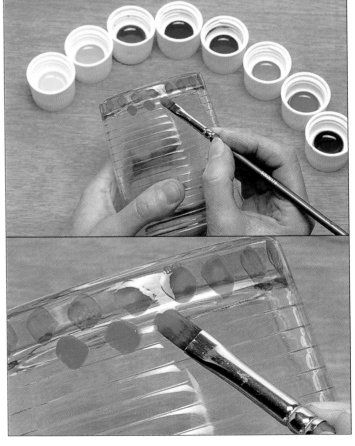

4 Continue in this way with each color, finishing with a row of citrine squares about halfway up each glass. Paint the fruit bowls and jug to complete the set. The jug is bigger than the other items, so use the medium-sized brush in order to make larger brush strokes. Leave all the glassware to dry for 24 hours, then bake in the oven following the manufacturer's instructions.

## *artist's tip*

Another way to add interest to uncolored glass is to paint into any cut areas. The thick base of this glass has a star pattern and has been painted in alternate shades of blue and green. This could be left as the sole decoration or combined with other patterns in harmonizing colors. Use a small, pointed brush to reach into the indentations, then wipe across the surface to remove any excess paint and leave clean edges.

## *Variation*

Use a different palette of colors, perhaps to team with patterned china and table linen.

This salad set has a summery look and a charmingly hand-painted finish. The life-like daisies are very easy to paint using angled brushes to form the regular and naturalistic petals with single strokes. Dividing the plate and bowl into equal sections means you won't need to draw a pattern for this delightful design.

## You will need

citrine
ivory white
malachite

Glass plates and salad bowl
Small square brush
Water-based paints, such as Porcelaine 150, as shown above
Colored wax pencil
Ruler
Medium-sized round brush
Medium-sized angled brush
Piece of glass or acetate to practice on
Long-haired brush
Small angled brush
Cotton buds
Denatured alcohol

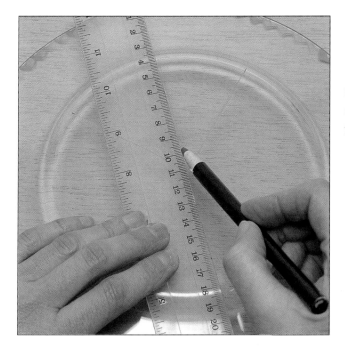

1 Clean the plates and bowl thoroughly. Using the small square brush and malachite, paint an even zigzag border around the edge of one of the plates. Make about three zigzags, then replenish the paint on the brush to keep the color even. If you make a mistake or the pattern becomes uneven, wipe it off quickly with a damp cloth. Leave to dry. Paint the remaining plates in the same way.

2 Using the wax pencil and the ruler, draw across the center of the first plate to divide it in half. Repeat the process to divide it into quarters and then eighths. The lines will help you to space the flowers evenly.

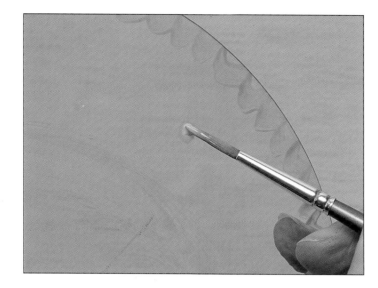

3 Using the medium-sized round brush and the citrine color, paint a solid circle level with the end of each line to form the flower centers. Paint each circle centrally on the raised edge of the plate to leave space around it for the petals. Leave to dry while you paint the remaining plates.

4 Using the white paint and medium-sized angled brush, practice painting the flower petals on a spare piece of glass or acetate. Dip just the tip of the brush into the paint, then place it on the glass with a single short dabbing motion. This will make a convincing petal shape each time and you should be able to paint two or three petals with one dip into the paint. The fullness and shape of the petals will vary according to the pressure you put on the brush.

5 Now paint the daisy petals onto the first plate. Put the first four petals opposite each other, turning the plate so that the point of the brush is always closest to the flower center. Then paint two petals in each gap. Continue in this way until you have eight complete daisies. Try to keep them the same size with the petals evenly spaced. Leave to dry while you paint the petals onto the remaining plates.

6 Working on the first plate, use the malachite paint and the long-haired brush to paint a linking stem between each daisy. Work from the inner to the outer edge of the plate and make the line curve naturally in a gentle S-shape. Turn the plate as you go so that you are always working from the outer edge of the plate. Use the same paint and brush to paint two short branches on each stem.

## artist's tip

If you find it difficult to keep your hand steady when painting on curved surfaces and larger objects like the salad bowl, rest it on a small box so that it is on the same level as the surface you are working on. You can also use pieces of kneadable adhesive to hold the object in place.

7 Go over the branches with a second coat of malachite if the original lines seem too pale.

8 Paint about ten small leaves around each branch, following the technique described in step 5 but using the small angled brush and malachite paint. Always point the brush towards the stem so that the leaves are the same shape. Paint the stems, branches and leaves onto the remaining plates, then decorate the salad bowl. Divide its base into sections, as in step 2, then extend the lines to the rim of the bowl and decorate in the same way as the plates. Leave the plates and bowl to dry, then remove the wax pencil marks with a cotton bud dipped in denatured alcohol. Bake in the oven following the manufacturer's instructions.

Each stroke made with an angled brush makes a single, very natural-looking petal or leaf shape. Try a similar design with multicolored flowers that look like gerberas rather than daisies.

# Mirrors, Frames and Candle Holders
# Gallery

**This page:**

Glass paints are ideal for adding a decorative, painted edging to plain glass or a mirror.

### Beaded Mirror
The round mirror shown here was masked using the template on page 92 to create a wavy edge sprayed with frosting. The edging is decorated with glued-on glass nuggets drizzled with silver outliner.

### Fabulous Frames
The pictures are mounted in inexpensive clip frames decorated with patterns drawn in outliner to create a frame effect. Black and silver was used to decorate the smaller frame. The larger one has a black grid with tourmaline pink detailing. When the outliner had dried, some areas were painted with deep blue transparent paint to complete the design and complement the picture.

**Opposite page:**

Candleholders are perfect for small beginner projects and make lovely gifts. They also sell very well at craft fairs and fundraising events.

### Flower Light
The flower-shaped holder is adorned with glued-on glass nuggets in matching colors and drizzled with gold outliner.

### Colorful Stars
The round candleholder was masked with self-adhesive stars and sprayed with frosting. Once the masks are peeled off, colour in the clear star shapes with oil-based paints.

### Swirls and Dots
Freehand lines, dots and spirals in gold outliner give a lovely effect on colored glass.

# Roman Vase

U se subtly colored porcelain paints to create an ancient Roman look for a vase. You will totally transform the surface of the glass so that it resembles an ancient, blue-green opaline finish, shaded with pewter and gold.

*1* Clean the vase thoroughly. Spread the paints onto a palette and, starting at the top edge of the vase, sponge on some of the opaline green onto one side of the vase, working down toward the base. Add some of the turquoise near the rim and blend it carefully with the lighter color. The small bubbles that appear on the surface will dry to create the texture needed. Set the vase aside until touch-dry, then paint the other side. Leave until touch-dry.

**2** Experiment with the different shades on a spare piece of glass or acetate. Use small pieces of synthetic sponge to apply the colors with a firm dabbing motion and blend them together as you work around the vase.

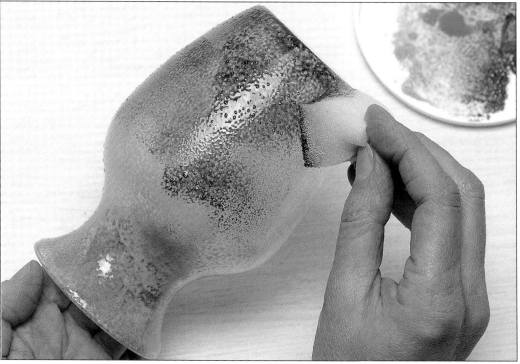

**3** Turn the vase around again and sponge a light coating of pewter around the base, shading it up the sides. Blend this with some of the blue-green so that the colors merge. Leave until touch-dry.

### artist's tip

Use this technique with different colors as the base for an opulent gold or silver design similar to Venetian glassware. Terracotta mixed with copper, or pinks with a pearl finish would look particularly good.

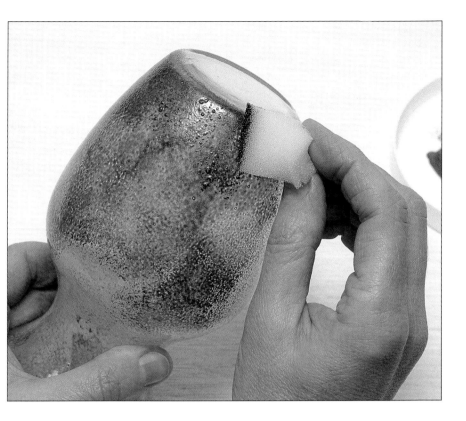

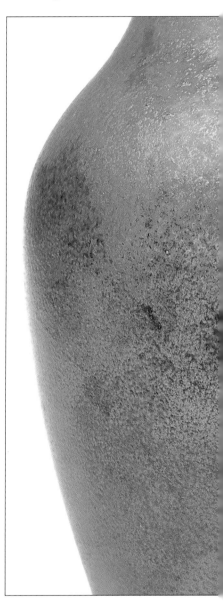

Try to achieve perfect blending of the
blues and greens for best results.

4 Using a clean piece of sponge, add
some more pewter color near the
base of the vase to darken it and
accentuate the metallic finish. Leave until
touch-dry.

5 Pour a little gold paint onto a clean
palette. Using a clean piece of
sponge, add subtle gold highlights
over the blue-green areas, concentrating the
color on the shoulder and rim of the vase.
Leave to dry completely. Bake in the oven
following the manufacturer's instructions.

# 14 PROJECT Beaded Blind

L arge, plain glass beads are reasonably priced and fun to decorate. You can easily produce hand-colored ones to match your fabric, and they will cost a fraction of what you would pay in a shop. When you have painted a collection of beads with different designs, thread them together to create a highly individual, beaded fringe that will catch the light and make the colors glow. Simple spots and stripes are very effective while marbled and dipped versions also look good.

## You will need

emerald
green-gold
lemon
turquoise
dark blue
yellow

Large oval glass beads
Large flat glass beads
Smaller round
glass beads
Wooden skewers
Masking tape
Transparent glass
paints, as shown above
Long-haired brushes
Small round brushes
or cotton buds
Appropriate thinner
for cleaning brushes
Jar filled with sand
Large darning needle
Embroidery yarn or
fine cord
Fabric blind to decorate

*1* Clean the beads thoroughly. Push each bead onto a wooden skewer. The skewer will hold the bead so that you don't smudge the paint as you work. If the hole in the bead is too large, wind some masking tape around the top of the skewer to make it big enough to hold the bead firmly in place.

*2* For a one-color bead, simply dip it into the pot of paint and lift it out quickly. Allow any drops of paint to fall back into the pot, then leave the bead to dry on the skewer. Decorate some of the large beads in this way and all of the small ones. You can also create half-colored beads by dipping them halfway into the paint.

painting glass/project 14

*Variation*

Paint a varied range of designs and colors to make a lively and interesting fringe for a lampshade.

*3* Use the long-haired brush to paint even stripes on a selection of large beads. Coat the brush well with the paint, rest the tip of the brush on the widest point of the bead and then twist the skewer until the paint forms a stripe all around the middle. Leave to dry.

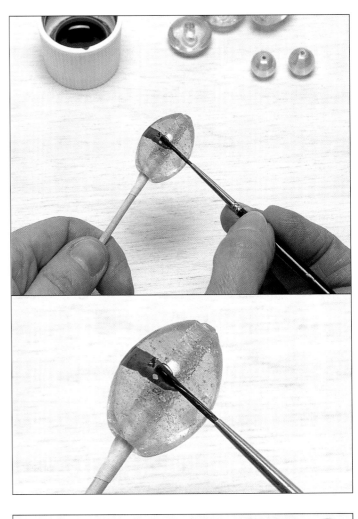

*4* Paint dots of all sizes on other large beads, using a small round brush or a cotton bud. You can paint them directly onto unpainted beads or add lines of dots to half-colored and striped designs once the paint has dried. Try dark contrasting dots on a bead dipped in a paler color. Leave all the beads to dry.

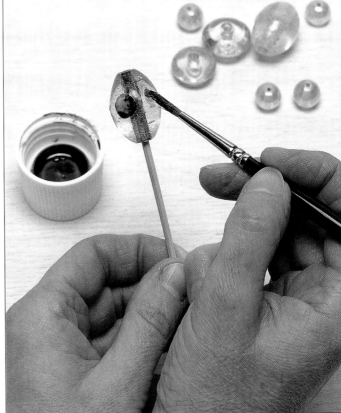

**5** To avoid smudging the wet paint, push the ends of the skewers into a jar filled with sand. This will hold the beads securely while the paint dries and enables you to view the range of colors and designs.

**6** To make the beads into a fringe for the blind, use the large darning needle to thread a few beads onto embroidery yarn or fine cord. Then thread on a small bead and take the yarn back through the other beads. With the needle still threaded, stitch both ends of the yarn into the back of the bottom edge of the blind. Knot the ends of the yarn together and trim them neatly. Make a fringe in this way, spacing the rows of beads evenly and varying the beads in each row.

painting glass/project 14                83

# Plates & Bowls
# Gallery

This page:

Plates are fun to decorate as their flat surfaces are easy to paint on. Try a single design as a decorative piece for display, or paint a whole set for a special table setting.

## Blue Frost
The blue frosted plate is decorated with matching glass nuggets glued evenly around the edge of the plate using glass bond. The area between each nugget is decorated with random, wavy lines of gold outliner.

## Marble Effect
The random mottled design on the underside of the plate is achieved using the marbling technique on page 16. Dark blue and violet oil-based paints blend well together using this method.

## Eastern Flavor
For the oriental design, tape a tracing of the characters on page 94 to the underside of the plate and follow the designs in black outliner on the surface of the plate. When dry, fill in with black water-based paint. Leave to dry and then sponge the underside of the plate's edge using gold water-based paint. Bake in the oven to make the design permanent.

Opposite page:

All the bowls are painted with oil-based paints and so can only be used as decorative pieces.

## Molded Swirls
Simply fill in the smooth surface around the molded pattern with chartreuse green and leave the molded lines clear.

## Fish Bowl (Artist: Vikki Miller)
The different fish shapes are painted freehand with oil-based paints in various colors. You can also draw your designs on paper, tape them inside the bowl and trace them with black outliner.

## Marbled Bowls
These two bowls were marbled following the instructions on page 16. Once dry, they were decorated with some gold sponging around the top edge and a "shoreline" of gold outliner.

## Flat Fish
The fins and scales on this molded fish dish were painted with a mix of blues and greens, to make a pretty dish for the bathroom.

# Art Deco
# Uplight

Art Deco is a classic, simple style that is ideal for this angular uplight. Soft, muted colors with black and frosted finishes provide an authentic look that is redolent of the 1930s. The shade can be made of clear plastic instead of glass, but remember that plastic cannot be baked in the oven as it will melt.

## You will need

anthracite
opaline green
lapis blue
ivory white

Glass or plastic
uplighter shade
Colored wax pencil
Ruler
Pencil
Paper
Narrow masking tape
Craft knife
Cotton buds
Denatured alcohol
Water-based paints,
such as Porcelaine
150, as shown above
Palette
Fan-shaped brush

**1** Clean the shade thoroughly. Mark the top edge of the holder on the shade with the wax pencil and then remove the holder. Trace the outline of the shade onto a sheet of paper. Draw the fan sections and an inverted V-shaped stripe on paper as shown, using ruler and pencil.

2 Measure and mark a central line on the shade using the ruler and wax pencil. Using the design you drew in step 1 as a guide, measure and mark the top point of the V-shaped stripe on this line.

3 Starting at the marked point on the central line, press a strip of masking tape out toward the left-hand edge of the shade. Repeat this on the other side to form an inverted V. Press the tape firmly into any indentations to keep the line straight, and run your finger over the edges of the tape to ensure the paint will not seep underneath it.

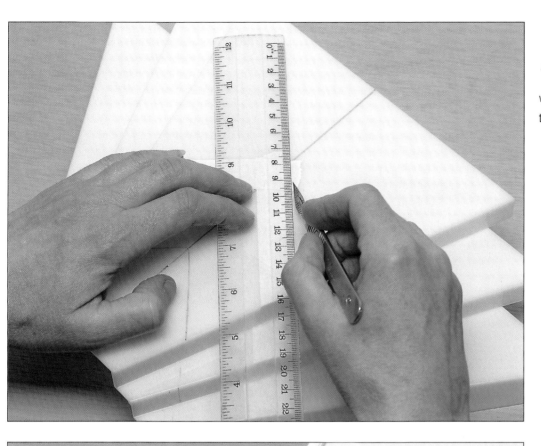

4 Using the ruler and craft knife, trim the masking tape into an accurate point where the layers overlap. Peel off the excess tape.

5 Leave a gap about twice the width of the masking tape, then apply two strips of tape, as in step 3, to make the top of the V. Remove the wax pencil mark with a cotton bud dipped in denatured alcohol. Pour a little of each color onto the palette and mix some opaline green with a little anthracite and ivory white to make a pale greeny-grey. Use this color and the fan-shaped brush to fill in the areas at the top of the shade and the top part of the inverted V-shape at the base. Dab the brush flat onto the surface of the shade, starting at the top in each area, and gradually work out from the center with a dabbing motion to make a regular, scalloped texture.

## 15 PROJECT

**6** Mix some of the lapis blue paint with the ivory white to make a pale blue and apply this in the same way to the middle stripe. Leave to dry.

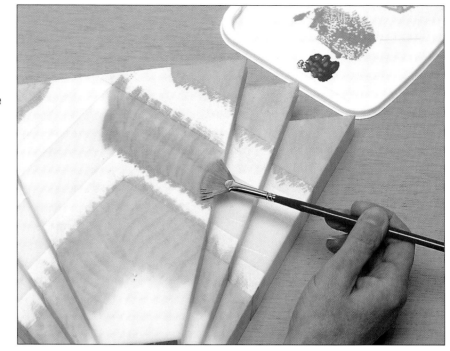

**7** Carefully peel off the masking tape to reveal the painted stripes. If the tape starts to pull off the paint in some places, run the tip of the craft knife along its edge to cut through the layer of paint, then peel off the tape.

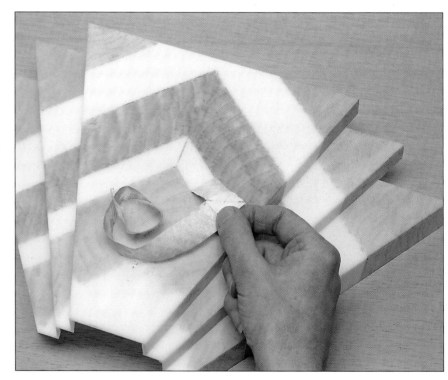

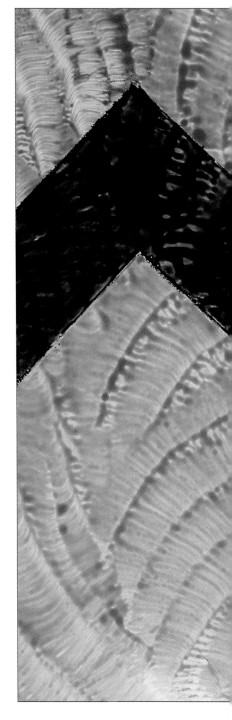

**8** Rub out the remainder of the wax pencil line with a cotton bud dipped in denatured alcohol. When the paint is completely dry, lightly press strips of masking tape onto either side of the unpainted stripe in the center of the shade, following the instructions in step 3.

Note the delicate, scalloped texture achieved with the fan-shaped brush. For perfect results, practice the dabbing motion necessary to create this effect on a piece of spare glass or acetate.

**9** Paint the central stripe with the anthracite color and fan-shaped brush, using the dabbing technique described in step 5 to create a scalloped texture. Leave to dry, then peel off the tape as in step 7. Bake in the oven, following the manufacturer's instructions, but only if you have used a glass – and not a plastic – shade. Attach the holder to the uplight.

# Templates

Strawberry Glass
Red stencil
(see page 40)

Swedish-style
Wine Glasses
(see page 60)

Strawberry Glass
Green stencil
(see page 40)

Beaded Mirror
(see page 74)
Enlarge to fit
your mirror size

Lightcatchers
(see pages 64-65)

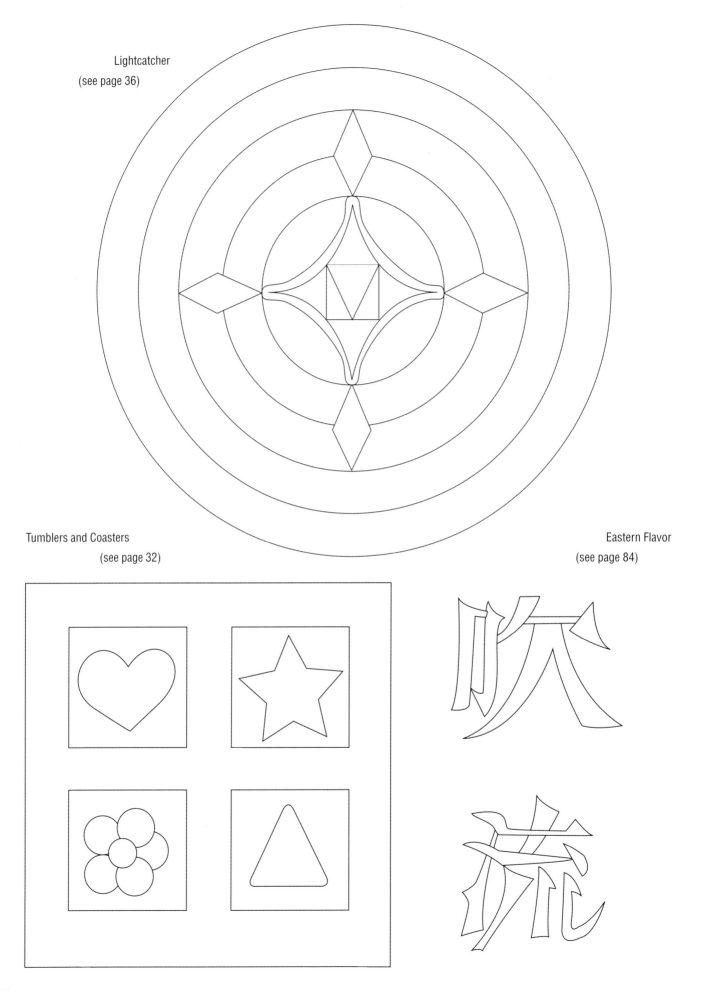

Lightcatcher
(see page 36)

Tumblers and Coasters
(see page 32)

Eastern Flavor
(see page 84)

94

# Suppliers and Acknowledgements

**DecoArt**
Box 386
Hwy Jct 150 & 27
Stanford, KY 40484
www.decoart.com
(800) 367-3047
(paint supplier)

**Delta Technical Coatings**
2550 Pellissier Pl
Whittier, CA 90601
www.deltacrafts.com
(800) 423-4135
(paint supplier)

**Gem Craft, Inc.**
1590 NW 159th Street
Miami, FL 33169
1-800-627-0820
(paint supplier)

**Pebeo of America**
Rt. 78, Airport Rd
Swanton, BT 05488
(819) 829-5012
www.pebeo.com
(paint supplier)

**Plaid Enterprises, Inc.**
P.O. Box 7600
Norcross, GA 30091-7600
1-800-842-4197
www.plaidonline.com
(paint supplier)

**ACKNOWLEDGEMENTS**

Many thanks to John Wright of
Pebeo UK for the generous supply of
different paints and outliners that have
been used extensively in this book and to
Carol Hook of Clear Communications Ltd
for all her help and information on the
products provided.
Also grateful thanks to Sue McIldowie,
Vikki Miller and Annette Malbon for
allowing me to show some of their glass
painting work in the gallery sections of
the book.

# Index

3-dimensional effect/texture 16, 42

**A**
abstract pattern (moulded) 21
acetate
    shapes 45
    stencil 60
Art Deco uplighter 86

**B**
baking
    outliners *see* water-based paints
    water-based paints 10-12
Beaded blind 80
blending colors 13, 14
Blue and gold glassware 50
Bottles and vases gallery 30
bowls 84-85
brushes 8
    angled 13
    cleaning 10, 12
    fan-shaped 13, 89
    flat 13
    long-haired 13
    round 13

**C**
Candle and tea-light holders 56
candle holders 74-75
chinagraph (wax) pencil 10
Christmas decorations 64
cleaning
    brushes 10, 24
    glassware 8
    grease off glass 8, 27
    natural sponges 14
cocktail sticks/wooden skewers 10
color schemes 17
comb (for patterns) 44
cotton buds 10
crackle finish 16
craft knife 10
crazy patchwork 30

**D**
denatured alcohol 8
design inspiration 17

**E**
edging 13, 74
embedding (into gel paints) 12
excess (removing)
    paint 63
    spray 34

**F**
Flora and fauna gallery 54
Flowery salad plates and bowl 70
foam applicator 14
frames 74
frosted colors 12
frosted (etched) designs 15, 32, 84
frosting spray 12

**G**
gel, using 16
    as glue 16
gel paints 12
glass adhesive 16, 38
glass beads 80
glass cutter 10
Glasses gallery 40
glass nuggets 16, 45, 58, 74, 84
glassware
    baking/firing 10-12
    for painting 8
glue gun 16

**H**
hanging
    lightcatchers 29, 64
    night-light holders 25
Hurricane Lamp 46

**I**
inspiration 17

**L**
labels, removing sticky residue 22
leaves 13, 54
Lightcatchers 36
Lightcatchers gallery 64
lining (with color) 30

**M**
marbling 16, 84, 85
masking 15
masking fluid 58
masking tape 10, 15, 48, 50, 57, 88
matte
    finish 10
    medium 12, 15, 40, 62
    varnish 12
metallic finish 79
mineral spirits 12
Mirrors, frames and candle holders 74
mixing paints 24
    with thinners 25
molded designs 19, 40, 84-85
Molded bottles and jars 18

**O**
oil-based paints 10
outliners 12, 27, 50
    using 15

**P**
pastel effect 12
Perfume Bottles 26
petals 13, 54, 70-72
plant stems and tendrils 13, 21, 73
Plates and bowls gallery 84
practice jars 28

**R**
Rainbow jug, tumblers and bowls 66
relief outliners *see* outliners
Roman vase 76

**S**
scratching designs 15
solvents 8
spatulas 10
sponges 10
    natural 13
    synthetic 14
sponging 48-48, 57, 77-79
Square Flower Vases 42
Stained Glass Night Lights 22
stencilling 12, 14, 40, 60-63
Swedish-style wine glasses 60

**T**
templates, making 53
texture 12, 13, 14, 42-44, 89, 91
Tiffany glass effect 12
Tumblers and coasters 32

**V**
Venetian style 40, 50, 78

**W**
water-based enamel paints 12
water-based paints 10
    firing/baking 10-12
wave pattern 44
wax pencil see Chinagraph pen